LYRICS OF LOVE

By

Elvin Blake Primm

Copyright © 2021 **Primm Publishing**

All rights reserved. No part of this publication may be reproduced, distributed, or transmitted in any form or by any means, including photocopying, recording, or other electronic or mechanical methods, without the prior written permission of the publisher, except in the case of brief quotations embodied in critical reviews and certain other noncommercial uses permitted by copyright law. For permission requests, write to the publisher, addressed "Attention: Book Rights and Permission," at the address below.

Published in the United States of America

ISBN 978-1-955243-84-1 (SC)
ISBN 978-1-955243-85-8 (Ebook)

Primm Publishing
7209 Lady Ann Ct,
Charlotte, NC 28216, USA
www.stellarliterary.com

Order Information and Rights Permission:

Quantity sales. Special discounts might be available on quantity purchases by corporations, associations, and others. For details, contact the publisher at the address above.

For Book Rights Adaptation and other Rights Permission. Call us at toll-free 1-888-945-8513 or send us an email at admin@stellarliterary.com.

Contents

WELCOME TO THE PLEASURE ZONE 1
THE LICKING STICK 3
THE LICKING STICK (PART 2) 5
OOOOOO......AHHHHH 7
DARKNESS OF THE NIGHT 9
VOLUPTUOUS 11
EVENING OF MARCH 25TH 13
AFTER THOUGHT 15
GETTING SOME 17
HOW I FEEL 19
GIVE ME SOME OF THAT CHOCOLATE CAKE 21
4:30 IN THE MORNING 23
THE LAST TIME I SAW YOU 25
RECOVERING FROM LOVE 27
THOUGHTS 29
HELP ME TO PUT OUT THE FIRE 31
MIDNIGHT REFLECTIONS 33
UNSAID WORDS 35
NOT FEELING THIS ANY MORE 37
MORNNG, NOON, AND NIGHT 39
MID DAY THOUGHTS ON THE JOB 41
The Widow (Widower's) Tribute 43
HEAVENLY BLISS 45
HAVE IT IN THE ROUGH 47
TWO BODIES COMING TOGETHER AS ONE 48

EUPHORIA	50
JUICY FRUIT	52
TWO O'CLOCK IN THE DAMN MORNING	54
BLACK PANTS AND TIGHT THIGHS	56
CANDY CANE	58
Get you from behind	60
FEELINGS WE WILL NEVER HIDE	62
SEXUAL ESCAPADE	64
FAREWELL LETTER	66
PASSION IN THE RAIN	68
I'LL BE WAITING FOR YOU	70
INFATUATED	72
A KISS BEFORE YOU GO	74
TONIGHT IS THE NIGHT	76
LATE NIGHT FANTASY	78
IN THE ROMANTIC MOOD	80
I DON'T WANT NOBODY ELSE	82
LET'S MAKE LOVE	84
WHEN I'M AROUND YOU	86
I WANNA MAKE LOVE TO YOU	88
WHY CAN'T WE TRY, ONE MORE TIME	90
COMING HOME	92
I NEVER KNEW WHAT LOVE WAS	94

WELCOME TO THE PLEASURE ZONE

Welcome to the Pleasure Zone,

Where erotica has found a home.

A place where all your fantasies do come true,

Let's take a trip there, just me and you.

All of the love that we've been making,

Full out passion, with bodies aching.

Soft and tender is your skin,

I search for the woman deep within…. your soul.

Chocolate syrup smeared across your lips,

Golden honey dripping from your finger tips.

Ice cubes used to quench your fire,

Whip cream to intensify the desire.

Step right up and spin the wheel,

When it stops you can cop a feel.

Tie me up or tie me down, if it turns you on

Blind fold over my eyes as you tease me until the dawn.

Lingerie of silk and satin with a touch of lace,

Clings against your body, your nails caress my face.

Ever so gently caressing me from head to toe,

Making my body tremble as I beg for more.

As we come to the end of this wild ride,

The climax is sensual like the look in your eyes.

Where you'll get off, no one knows,

The sensation never ends, as it continues to grow.

All that you've desired and kept in your mind

Will be like a wild fire, burning until the end of time.

Welcome to the Pleasure Zone,

Where erotica has found a home.

THE LICKING STICK

I once knew a girl named Nikki,

She always loved things that were sticky.

But when she wanted to get her freaky kicks,

She got it on with her Licking Sticks.

She had them in all shapes and sizes,

Colors and even with multiple flavors.

But she loved the one with the chocolate and cream,

If you saw her work it, you'd know what I mean.

She licks it like it was going out of style,

Her tongue and lips always going wild.

Drooling and slurping like that thang was real good,

Making a brother hard as hell just like she knew she would.

Then she would take it and rub it between her breasts,

With her other hand was a towel to clean up her sexy mess.

That she would make when she puts the stick in between her thighs,

As her juices flowed, she would roll back her eyes.

As the licking stick would penetrate her and make her lips vibrate,

Make a man want to be the stick just so he can ejaculate,

When the licking stick went all the way in…..

Nikki would start the erotic fun all over again.

THE LICKING STICK (PART 2)

The licking stick, the licking stick

My baby loves her licking stick.

If you saw her playing with it you'd understand why,

It definitely is a sight for only your eyes.

When she puts it in her mouth and gets it all wet,

She starts moaning and groaning as if she is trying to get

To a Tootsie pop and take out the center.

Sounding like the licking stick has just entered.

Her wet mound of goodness and cream,

That has gotten soaked like an erotic wet dream.

Then she takes the licking stick and sticks it in,

And allows all of the real fun to begin.

She slides the stick in and out,

Moaning and groaning and leaving no doubt.

That she's enjoying that big Ol' Dick,

That thing she calls her licking stick.

When she is done and has come over and over again,

She grabs that stick and places it in.

Her mouth and begins to suck it dry,

Her Licking stick will never die.

OOOOOO……AHHHHH

When you say OOOOO…..AHHHHH

It makes my body yearn for you.

When you say OOOOO…..AHHHHH

It makes my fire burn for you.

When we're making love all night

You know how to treat me right.

When I know I have hit that spot,

That moan tells me what is what!

To see your eyes roll back in your head

Lets me know that you know it too.

When we're finished doing the do,

You lay there all sexy in my bed sayin'

OOOOO…….AHHHHH!!!

OOOOO…….AHHHHH!!!

When you caress my manhood,

With your tongue and your hands

Everything inside me understands

That yes, you are that damn good !!!!

Got me saying , OOOOO……AHHHHH !!!

DARKNESS OF THE NIGHT

In the darkness of the night…

The visions in my mind can see,

Me loving you and you loving me.

In the darkness of the night….

As my eyes are closed tight,

But my mind is open wide

Allowing all of my thoughts to collide.

Fused together and to become one,

The rush of joy and the feeling of ecstasy

The climatic state my mind can see

Bringing together the taste of love that has us both over come.

The sensations of the darkness of night,

Always seem to rise.

In the darkness of the night,

As I look into your eyes.

The passion that we both release,

Is the type that is envied by all.

In the moment of all of our peace,

I always hearken to your call.

In the darkness of the night,

We can be all that we want to be.

I always want you to be a part of me,

In the darkness of the night.

VOLUPTUOUS

As I stare at you lying in my bed

You're sleeping so sound and cool.

While erotic visions run through my head,

Making me want to act a fool.

Your delicious curves stand out in the night,

While I admire your silhouette.

My desires and intentions go from wrong to right,

Wanting all of what you have if you'd just let.

Me, just run my hands up and down

Your heavenly body and your beautiful hair.

As I touch you in certain spots you start to make sounds,

You turn and face me and our eyes begin to stare.

Into one another as we start the fore play,

Of another erotic and tasty forum.

I want to always and forever stay,

Locked into your beautiful decorum.

As voluptuous as you are my mind has been overcome,

The needs that have risen up in us.

I want to always be able to enjoy me some,

Of you and everything that makes you voluptuous.

EVENING OF MARCH 25TH

Feeling the pain and the agony,

That has been handed to me .

To know that he has you tonight,

At this moment it just doesn't feel right.

Last night a full twenty four hours ago,

You were lying in my arms.

Telling me how you felt as we made love , so,

Passionately and romantically as I filled you with my charms.

But now you are being wined and dined,

He's probably holding you by the lake.

The attention he's giving you now is truly fake,

I'm the one whose really on your mind.

All I want to do is scream,

Because deep down inside I know how I feel.

You always tell me how much I mean,

To you, but from him you can't seem to peel.

Yourself away from his lies and deceptions,

Even though deep down you want his affection.

I've been a decoy and a way for you to leave,

Until a certain time, then you allow me to believe.

That I'm truly the man that you want,

That I'm the man you need.

So I'm going forward don't taunt,

As my heart continues to bleed.

AFTER THOUGHT

Another night has come and gone,

As I watch you in front of the bed.

We had one hell of a night and it was on,

Erotic visions run through my head.

The stains on the sheets are a reflection,

Of the hours we spent together.

As I lay here and think of the perfection,

Of a night that continued to get better and better.

The tenderness that was felt over and over again,

The affection that was displayed every minute.

To be able to feel it from the start to the end,

Makes me feel ecstatic that I was up in it.

All the goodness and sensual love you gave,

To me until my toes curled and eyes rolled.

Made me feel like a love slave,

All that good loving has taken a toll.

On my mental and physical self,

To the point that I'm set free.

I want to place your love in a bottle and place on a shelf.

And open it when I'm alone and let it do me.

As the twilight comes and you crawl into bed,

And snuggle down beside me.

Your hands are wrapped around my head,

As we take each other to the land of ecstasy.

GETTING SOME

Pour the champagne into the glass,

While I get the baby oil and tap that ass.

You said you were mine, yes I'm very possessive,

As I raise your legs up and be aggressive.

When you told me that your ass was mine,

I cherish it like roses on Saint Valentine.

Flip it over, turn around and let it bounce,

As I slip the anaconda in and give you every ounce.

You give me reasons to make love to you,

Into the night and the early morn.

If you only knew all the things I want to do,

It would be rated X and an all time porn.

Take the lollipop and put it in your mouth,

In and out, in and out in slow motion,

Then I push back and put my tongue down south,

And watch you squirm and moan in commotion.

This starts to feel like an eternity,

Until we both climax together.

We lay in the bed hot and sweaty,

Hoping the next time will be even better.

HOW I FEEL

Is this for real?

The feelings that I feel.

Every time I'm near you,

My heart wants to endear you.

The feelings that I feel,

Are alive and for real.

The tears that are in my eyes,

Come from the love that's come alive.

You and I must stop this moment of confusion,

Because what we have is not an illusion.

In my mind you will ever be,

The only one that is for me.

When the stars above are align,

I always have you on my mind.

Just something I can't explain,

I get goose bumps from the sound of your name.

I pray to God that He gave,

To me someone that I can embrace.

As I pour my heart out on my sleeve,

That my love is real and not make believe.

As I conclude and tell you this,

Can't wait to embrace and gently kiss

Those lips that speak so softly to me

I love and adore you don't ever leave.

GIVE ME SOME OF THAT CHOCOLATE CAKE

Give me some of that chocolate cake

As you take it out of the pan

All I want to do is partake

Of all the goodness I can stand.

Give me some of that chocolate cake

As your icing melts from your fingers

And I lick that batter that you make

And make your orgasms linger and linger.

As I put my fork deep into you

Can't believe how tender and moist

The thickness that is you

Your shape, your tenderness, your voice.

As I cut into your tender thighs

And see the rolling back of your eyes

My manhood begins to swell

As I try to beat that thing like hell.

The lickity lick of your sweetness

And all that chocolate thunder

Is truly the sign of my weakness

And all that you possess under.

That short skirt and your thick legs

Keeping a brother always on the beg

Give me some of that chocolate cake

So we can get in on baby, this is no mistake.

Give me some of that chocolate cake.

4:30 IN THE MORNING

As I partake of this ass at 4:30 in the morning

Looking forward to hearing you moaning and groaning

Watching your head go up and down

On my joy stick of pleasure, you going round and round.

I have my hand on the back of your head,

And I slowly move down to caress your back

You move in anticipation of the erotic thoughts of exhilaration

As you move yourself to the other side of the bed

I get up and position myself on top to lay it down with no slack.

As I thrust my stuff up inside you and your wetness

Your reflexes make you jump and squirm

The pussy feels good and I will never forget this

Come on baby get a taste of this sperm.

After thumping and bumping it gets better with every stroke

Like lighting up a joint and getting high at every toke.

The sounds that you make as I get deep inside of you,

Drives me crazy baby as I continue to do you.

I move down to your hot box and begin to lick

It starts to drive you crazy just like my joy stick

The tongue moving in and out and all around

As I look up you're rubbing your nipples and making those sounds.

You want to cum so bad that you are about to scream

I rise up and place my stuff back inside

Knocking that thing up and you begin to cream

All over big daddy as he slips and slides.

THE LAST TIME I SAW YOU

Soft brown hair and lips so tender,

Skin so fair making my emotions surrender.

To the beauty that you have displayed over the years,

Bringing a grown man to drown in his tears.

As I lay awake at night in a haze,

As the hours pass it seems like days.

I get excited thinking of all the things you do,

Since the last time I saw you.

I toss and turn while my insides burn,

And it is your touch that I yearn for.

I think about the clothes you wear.

I think about the style of your hair and everything else I adore.

I feel the electricity from your body,

As I lay in my bed with sweat.

Everything is getting kind of foggy,

But I know that I'm not in Heaven yet.

Your love is in the realm of a different zone,

As I tried to make your body my own.

Too many times I get excited as I lay in your arms,

Waiting anxiously to be filled by your charms.

As the sun is coming up over the night,

And I'm groggy but full of delight.

Knowing those hours of distraught and pain,

Could never ever be restrained.

Since, the last time I saw you.

RECOVERING FROM LOVE

I can't take the rain,

When it's falling.

It reminds me of the pain,

Every time when I'm calling.

The drops look like tears,

Reminiscent of my lonely years.

Tearing my insides out,

Leaving me in doubt.

I cried that day,

After you were gone.

I waited for you to go away,

To let out how it felt being alone.

As the water cleans the street,

And my tears run down my face.

Someone good is who I pray that I'll meet,

And your ways will vanish without a trace.

One day my sun will shine,

And this person shall be mine.

We'll be more than friends,

And be together until the end.

Just like a wounded dove

I'll be recovering from love.

Flying higher and stronger,

My heart will no longer hunger.

For a love that doesn't exist,

And disappears like a mist.

Yes, the one I'm thinking of,

Will help me to recover from love.

THOUGHTS

Tell me how you feel when I'm around

Are you happy, sad or start to feel down?

This is something I need to know,

In order for my true feelings to show.

Fancy threads only make a man, what he fantasizes to be.

But I only want you to understand that I'm only being me.

I see you while I'm working, from the corner of my eye.

My senses continue lurking, as I try to read your mind.

I'd really like to get to know you, but I'm taking my time.

I know you are too, but one day you will be mine.

It may sound like I'm delaying, with all of the words I'm saying.

But let us keep cool for awhile, as

I continue enjoying your sweet smile.

Don't talk I want to look deep into your eyes,

And see if I can read the thoughts in your mind.

Certain things can come as a surprise,

It's amazing just how time flies.

I know that you'll be mine,

Because I know there is a sign.

Telling me everything will be alright,

So please be mine tonight.

Give me your love that is so sweet,

I want to kiss your lips right away.

Until our lips meet,

It will seem like forever and a day.

HELP ME TO PUT OUT THE FIRE

Oh!!!! Can you blame me for falling for you?

There is no shame in me, when I'm calling out for you.

In the middle of the night , as I lie awake tossing and turning.

It's my feelings that I'm fighting,

while my emotions constantly are burning.

If I get my hands on you, I don't know just what I'll do.

But you can sure bet, all of this good loving is what you'll get.

Help me put out the fire, before my insides burn out.

Help me put out the fire, so my soul can scream and shout.

When you walk in the room,I know the passion will start soon.

When you take off the negligee',

It's the start of a long and erotic day.

It might help if you left on the high heel shoes,

The high heels effect can never lose.

Leave the ruby red on the lips,

Get the champagne and let's have a sip.

Get an ice cube and I'll rub your back.

Up and down on the body that is intact.

Rolling around on the satin sheets,

While we make love, and listen to our hearts beat.

Just like a flame that is burning out of control,

You keep creeping into my soul.

Igniting the sparks that light the midnight sky,

And quenching the heat with a look from your eye.

If you help me put out the fire,

You'll take out the burning desire.

That stays lit twenty-four by seven,

As this experience will make us feel like heaven.

Like angels we'll fly and be eternally free,

So come, help put out the fire in me.

MIDNIGHT REFLECTIONS

Baby, I'm losing my focus

Because of all the things you do.

I was hoping that you wouldn't notice,

But every word I said was very true.

The way you do that thing with your tongue

It just drives me crazy and makes me wild.

Licking up and down on my pole as if you are having fun,

As I watch you look up at me with those eyes, makes me smile.

As my eyes roll back into my head,

Enjoying every stroke that you bring

All I want to do is get you in my bed,

And continue this while I make you sing.

As I place your legs on my shoulders and go down

On you and look up and watch you squirm,

I go deeper and deeper and enjoy all of your sounds

Of you moaning and groaning while your insides burn.

I slowly move up and place my stuff in you

You arch your back and moan with pleasure

As you take me inside you and let me do

Everything that you desire and open you like a buried treasure.

As the night fires burn for the two of us

The eternal flame dances in an erotic light

Allowing for the feelings of ecstasy and lust

We climax together and sleep into the good night.

UNSAID WORDS

As we make love into the eternal night

I stare deep into your luscious brown eyes

Unlimited moments that we share that might

Bringing thoughts of ecstasy and positions of compromise.

I caress your chocolate creamy thighs with my hands

And your reaction is so intense,

Without speaking we both understand

That a wonderful night is about to commence.

As we move into different positions

And enjoy each other with delight

Our love that we have has a definition

That no author could ever write.

The motion of your hips as they continue move

Back and forth while in between the sheets

Quietly acknowledging the steady flow of our groove

We have with each other and never off beat.

As the night turns to day and in due time

I stare at you and just admire

With the thoughts of last night playing in my mind

And the lustful thoughts of desire.

You turn to me and nod your head

And we smile at each other

Understanding without words unsaid

That we will be forever lovers.

NOT FEELING THIS ANY MORE

Every night when I come home,

I get this feeling like I am alone.

Even though you're lying here with me,

I know there's some place else I'd rather be.

My heart and mind are not in synch, The way they used to be.

Every time when I stop and think,

Deep inside it is hurting me.

I want to tell you so bad just how I feel, But I am afraid that you would never understand.

That someone else has my heart sealed,

Please forgive me, this was not planned.

I need to have the feeling of protection,

Can't continue with these feelings of rejection.

You always say that we can't find the time,

We're all grown now, do you think that I am blind?

That I can't see that you are leading me on,

Leaving me to feel like such a fool.

To make me think that we had something in common,

Only to be sucked away in a whirl pool.

That is only the beginning on how I feel

,I really feel like I want to roll out the door.

But, for now my lips will stay sealed,

Because, I am not feeling this anymore.

MORNNG, NOON, AND NIGHT

Every time I touch down there,

Filthy thoughts run thru my mind.

My fingers running thru your hairs,

I see your hips bump and grind.

My fingers caress you up and down,

While in the faint darkness of night.

I love to hear your moaning sounds,

Into the early morning light.

Slapping that ass until the early morn,

Into the bed room is where we'll adjourn.

Making that noise that you always do,

While I am popping that thang all up in you.

You like when I tap that ass,

Because you know I do it right.

I can really make it last,

Morning, noon and night.

I love to watch as your eyes roll back,

When I go downtown on you .

The others you've had, never did that,

It's a shame, they missed an erotic view.

All I know is that your stuff is just right,

Makes me wanna be in it,

Morning, Noon and Night !!!

MID DAY THOUGHTS ON THE JOB

Its 3am, I'm awake and my loins are burning,

As I touch myself and just imagine being with you.

My desires are on fire and they are yearning,

To get inside you and do what we do.

The thoughts of caressing your breasts,

And putting them in my mouth.

Makes me go into cardiac arrest,

As I proceed to go south.

The moisture you have in between those lips,

Arouses me to such an extreme.

When my tongue hits there, you grind your hips,

Makes me work it so much, it makes you scream.

I want to call but, you're probably a sleep,

Hopefully dreaming the same naughty thoughts.

I am picturing me in you so deep,

Mmmm, the images are making me raw.

I need to feed this hunger I have inside,

Gotta make love to you at this moment.

The feeling I get when I let you ride,

Is beyond words with this beautiful woman.

Maybe if I text you in our usual code,

You'll understand what I am trying to say.

The thought of sexing you creates a mode, That will last until the early day.

But to my dismay, I have made a mess. My hands are sticky and about to dry.

With all those arousing thoughts, I am no longer stressed.

Leaving me relieved and a peaceful sleep in my eyes.

The Widow (Widower's) Tribute

What do you do when someone you love is no longer there?

Do you forget that they even existed…act like you don't care?

Do you lie awake at night crying until you pass out and sleep?

Or do you wallow in pity and depression real deep?

Words can not describe how I truly feel about you.

Since you've been gone my life hasn't been the same.

I still feel like I am a part of you,

I still shed tears at the mention of your name.

I can still remember the first time we met,

You stood out amongst all of the others.

Treated me with the utmost respect,

That's how I knew we could be lovers.

As time went on, a family we did make.

We had our trials and tribulations but succeeded.

We did what no one said was possible, which was give and take,

During which time we defeated.

All the naysayers and doubters who thought they knew,

How to run our lives and tell us what to do.

When all along we had it all under control,

You were my rock, my anchor, the key to my soul.

Just when we thought we were on our way,

Something happened to my very best friend.

The Lord called you home and took you away,

That's when my world came to an end.

HEAVENLY BLISS

What are you waiting for?

Don't you want this?

Go on and close the door,

Let's enjoy this heavenly bliss.

Let me help you get undressed,

At the same time you do it for me.

Along the way I will gently caress,

All of your parts that are so lovely.

When we get down to our underwear,

I want to pull yours down with my tongue.

I promise to do it with delicate care,

Making you tingle when I'm done.

Lay you down on the bed,

With the candles burning in the night.

We're in the sixty nine position giving head,

To each other as we enjoy the delight.

Side to side, missionary, get you from behind,

Non stop love making, with no limits of time.

Sweating profusely as we do it all over again,

And knowing for sure, that it will never end.

HAVE IT IN THE ROUGH

I know you wanna do this baby,

But I'm not sure that you are ready.

I want to treat you like a lady,

Making love to you can be pretty steady.

Giving it to you the way I want to,

As I stop to look and stare.

The way you look up when we do the do,

Please don't stop it, if you dare.

Watching you lying here in the buff,

Makes me want you more and more.

But when we're doing it in the rough,

We can move it to the floor.

TWO BODIES COMING TOGETHER AS ONE

Two bodies coming together as one,

During a time when the day is done.

Her on him and him in her,

Will definitely create quite a stir.

While filling the room with the sounds of pleasure,

And the aromatic smell of love that they will treasure.

Two bodies coming together as one.

Her touching him, him holding her.

Reaching that climatic moment before the dawning of the sun.

Making love so often, that their minds and bodies are in a blur.

Hearts beating in unison, souls constantly colliding.

He looks up at her as she continues riding.

Two bodies coming together as one.

Perspiration dripping from them on to the bed.

Gripping the sheets and each other before they come.

To the ecstasy of climax that will rush to their head.

With the two bodies rubbing together causing friction.

Burning a hole in the mattress that they lay upon.

Two bodies coming together as one,

Tell the stories that are made in between the sheets.

Making novels that only the two will ever read.

Page by page tell of erotic moments filled with passion.

While the individuals unravel themselves in usual fashion.

Two bodies coming together as one,

Until next time…. this poem is done.

EUPHORIA

The intensity of how she goes down on ya,

will never leave a frown on ya.

So smooth and so divine, after you've tasted

her it will blow your mind.

The concoction of ecstasy will take your breath away,

Make you want more of her good stuff all day.

Once you've tasted the sweetness of her charms,

The bite that she gives will do you some harm.

Once you get behind her, she's very hard to hold,

Her sensual ways are a constant reminder that she is very bold.

Smooth to the touch is her fine ass,

You may like her warm but she is better when chilled.

Her figure is poured out like an hour glass,

With plenty of ecstasy to be fulfilled.

Once you are inside of her she will marinate,

Her mixture of her many juices will take your breath away.

If you don't tap out you will feel her fate,

As she flows through you she will escalate.

All of your inner inhibitions will come out,

Messing with your mind and leaving you in doubt.

The wonder of it all that will make you think,

How do you get all of that from one delicious drink.

JUICY FRUIT

When you have me in your mouth,

with all of my juices flowing

Deep throating me in and out until I am exploding.

Juices gushing everywhere, as you proceed to lick,

There's nothing left to even spare, from my chocolate stick.

You raise your head up from my lap,

when you've finished what you do

Around your lips and with a smack

you swallow all of the residue.

As you get up off your pretty knees,

I watch your lips start to quiver,

Your sexy eyes are begging me please

and your lips start to shiver.

You look as if you want me to put it in and do you all night,

As I proceed to fulfill your needs, I can feel those lips get tight.

The moisture that flows from your thong,

will make you take them off,

As I rise up in you hard and long,

all up in that stuff so hot and soft.

The feeling of me in you will make your hips rotate,

But as I am about to come you tell me "Hold up, wait"!

You push me back and throw your head down in lap once again,

To get a taste of what you like until the last drop ends.

TWO O'CLOCK IN THE DAMN MORNING

It's two o'clock in the damn morning

In a few hours the new day will be soon dawning.

I know my ass needs to be a sleep,

But this shit is so good and I'm in it real deep.

As usual baby your stuff is so damn good,

So moist and wet like I knew it would.

Should be illegal like smoking crack or weed,

That's why I am in it because it's just what I need.

Don't make no damn sense why this has my ass hooked,

My mind is so blown and my senses are totally shook.

When I look down at you as you roll those big brown eyes,

And just the thought of being in between those thick brown thighs.

Makes me wanna stay up in you all night ,

So soft and moist, everything is feeling just right.

I am sure you know just how good your stuff feels,

As I grab you by the ankles and hold you by your heels.

I am almost there and about to cum,

You push me back once again and get to your knees.

You suck my manhood down and swallow some,

As I lay there and watch you do it with such ease.

BLACK PANTS AND TIGHT THIGHS

Bring your ass over here

And let me feel on it my dear

While you have it packed in those black pants

You're making my manhood rise and stand.

I'm thinking about what I'll do to you

When I get you out of your clothes

There's so many nasty things I'll do

To you from your head to your toes.

Those thighs of yours are so thick

So luscious to the touch

I can't wait to get between them and stick

My rod up in you, I'm Jonesing for that very much.

And when I go downtown and make you squirm

All over my bed and as I put in the big worm

In between your moist mound and watch your eyes roll

As my manhood goes deeper into your soul.

You get on top and start to ride

As I caress your thick ass thighs

Getting up in you all night long

As my manhood continues to get strong.

To think it all started with them sexy ass black pants

When you strolled thru the door all fine and high

My inner man had to take a chance

To get them black pants off them thighs.

CANDY CANE

It was two in the morning and someone was texting

Talking about they're horny and need some sexing.

I responded back and with the quickness got dressed,

Thinking about that booty and I'm gonna unstress.

The pinned up feelings that you have inside

Making you come until the break of dawn.

I want that ass baby cause its been on my mind

When we get done with each other I'll roll over and watch you yawn.

Fall into a deep coma like sleep

With thoughts of me going up in you real deep

Tap you on the shoulder so I can get some

Don't give any attitude you know I wasn't done.

This time you get on top

Ride that dick baby until he pops.

When you watch him explode

Need you to lick up the entire load.

Kneeling and bobbing your head up and down

Make my head spin like a merry go round.

And when you're done we will do it over and over again

Because my baby can't get enough of this candy cane.

Get you from behind

Your ass up in the air, with your face down in the pillow.

Pulling on your sweaty hair as I drive deeper in your pussy willow.

Your back is arched at the perfect angle as I reach around,

And stroke your clit that's mangled in that sweet tasting mound.

I have my Johnson waiting to drive up in ya,

Like a big bad Caddy rolling out of Virginia.

I put him in and you begin to moan and groan,

Juices start flowing and he is still growing.

Riding and stroking, pounding and sticking

You getting hornier and hornier with this good dicking.

And just when I think I'm about to have some fun

You dip your hips trying to make a brother cum.

Sweat still dripping all down your back

And I'm still pounding on that ass.

While you back that thang up with no slack

I'm putting it to you trying to make it last.

Now we've finished laying it down

Only one thing comes to my mind

Every time that you come around

I'm going to get you from behind.

FEELINGS WE WILL NEVER HIDE

The sounds that you are truly making,

Display that there is no mistaking.

The screams of passion that we are partaking

And the orgasms that you're not faking.

This sweet music that I am hearing

As we make love it is so endearing

The harmonies that you are playing

While your luscious lips are gently saying.

Pillow talk that has its own rhythm

Your eyes roll back as I continue giving

All of me deep inside of all of you

As this moment we share continues

To reveal the erotic fantasies in our minds

As we explore deeper we lose track of time

So wrapped up into each other as we taste

The sweet nectar of each others fruits and waste ,

Not another moment worrying about those

From the past that left this undiscovered treasure

As we make sweet love and continue curling toes

The ecstasy we receive while giving each other pleasure.

Off into the next level of pure passion

And the end of our climatic ride

Our love making we will never ration

And our feelings for each other we will never hide.

SEXUAL ESCAPADE

Oh baby, only one thing I know for certain

Whatever you're doing is truly working

Not sure if you've done this thing before

I don't want you to stop, cause it only makes me want you more.

Feel it, touch it, stroke it, even lick

Whatever is clever just don't make it quick

Take your time and explore all of me

Bring that rush, make me hush, please baby please.

Good lovin' like this makes a grown man cry,

Every time we're together I always ask why ?

Why is it that you can do it like you do,

And then lay there and then I wonder who?

Who was this person that just turned me out

Got my insides screaming and about to shout.

Have me fiending like I'm on crack,

When all I want to do is blow out your back.

All I know is when I get a hold of you,

I want to travel deep inside you boo

Get inside all the erotic tales in your mind

As we come together and then press rewind.

Doing it all over and over again

Until the dawn of a new day.

I'm into you baby and I never want it to end.

But in reality we know it's a sexual escapade.

FAREWELL LETTER

In the arms of another is where you are

But from a distance, I continue to love you from a far.

As I reminisce about our final days

I can't help but feel confused by the way

You changed everything that I thought was you

The suspicions I had inside became unglued

Watching you unravel and fall a part

As I stood there with my bleeding heart

I couldn't believe how I let you back in

And try to play me and make me feel

Like I had no pride for myself as I begin

To put together all I lost and see you steal

The last breath and all my love I gave

Only to be set free and the lord did save

Me from your path of devious and destruction

I thank Him for His strength and direction.

While you lay in the arms of another

Always remember there will be no other

That will do for you as I did all the time

No matter how he makes you feel, I'm always on your mind.

As I close this letter out just know

That my life is better that you are gone

And as I continue to restore and grow

A distant memory you have become as I continue to move on.

PASSION IN THE RAIN

Tonight we'll find a new adventure,

That we know will never get censored.

The thoughts we have inside our heads,

Will come alive while we're here in bed.

As the rain continues to pour down outside,

The fires of passion heat up deep inside.

While we continue to take nothing for granted.

We've noticed that we've become hopeless romantics.

Tossing ideas back and forth,

The session is now par for the course.

Soaking wet with sensual desires,

Taking our game a little bit higher, is what we want to do.

Cascading in the homemade puddle we've made,

We end the passion with a passionate cuddle

As I move much closer to you.

I feel the beat of your pulse,

As it races then slows as a result.

Of the after math of our game,

You gently whisper my name.

With every breath you take,

I can feel your body tremble and shake.

Quivering like a new born baby,

I place a sheet over you.

To keep the warmth of this beautiful lady,

I'm so fortunate to have you.

I'LL BE WAITING FOR YOU

The night you went away, was the roughest night.

There was no other way, we were gonna make it right.

I tried to ask myself, what was the problem?

When I saw for myself, there was no way to solve them.

You told me we could be friends,

That didn't set in my heart too well.

You know I'll love you to the end,

Why must our love be a living hell?

I will be waiting for you, if you make up your mind.

I will be waiting for you, until the end of time.

You know there must've been some confusion,

Because we could never ever conversate.

So we came to one conclusion, that a life without love is irate.

The love I gave I thought was more than enough,

To keep you here for an eternity.

I know living with me was kind of rough,

But I didn't know you were full of uncertainty.

I will be waiting for you, I hope you come back soon.

I will be waiting for you, if you don't come back I'll be doomed.

Let's forget about the past, concentrate on the future.

I know my love can last, yours I'm not too sure.

Time may run out on you ,before our problems are solved.

But there's one thing that's true, for you my heart will stay involved.

INFATUATED

I still dream of you and I,

Back in the days when we were one.

That's when we were honest with no lies.

With no one else to call my own.

I can still see you embedded deep in my mind.

As clear as a bright sunny day.

It seemed like I spent all of my time,

With you because I didn't want you to get away.

But now time has placed us apart.

Far away so we'll never see.

What could've been you and me,

But every night I look to the stars.

Counting everyone as a part of our,

Many escapades that we encountered.

I know this won't bring back the hours,

But I feel like you're here forever.

As the full moon shines bright,

I picture your face at night.

Standing by the bay watching at a glance,

I still feel like we had a chance.

At a love but we'll never know.

Because love doesn't exist here any more.

A KISS BEFORE YOU GO

As the hands of time slowly wind down,

On our long weekend together.

I turn to you and see your frown,

As we stare at the stormy weather.

I walked over to try and console,

But you explained you were in control.

With your emotions and your inner thoughts,

Your sadness was like beauty in a picture forever caught.

Captured in the frame of my mind.

So that one day I'll be able to rewind.

This moment of heavenly and divine bliss,

Which was so gently sealed with a kiss.

A kiss before you go, is a keep sake embedded in my heart.

A kiss before you go, will always remain a wonderful part.

As you walk out that door,

I'll watch you as you leave.

Even though I'll be wanting more,

Your kiss will always stay with me.

The rain falls so heavily outside,

Just like the tears that fall from your eyes.

But as we approach the end of our rendez-vous,

I'll always be in love with you.

A kiss before you go, is all that I'll ever need.

It will let my spirit flow,

Even though my heart will continue to bleed.

TONIGHT IS THE NIGHT

As I continue to search your soul,

And uncover all your stories never told.

I hope to secure a place in your mind.

As I continue to search for the love of a lifetime.

Don't mistake my words as being hard,

Understand it's my heart I must guard.

With each day that continues to pass,

I'll continue to search for love that will last.

Tonight is the night I feel like being with you.

So turn out the lights, and show me what you want to do.

Tonight is the night to release the fury.

Of everlasting passion and continue to make history.

The mission that we have in our hands,

To make love until we understand.

That our purpose in life is to show affection,

For the one you love, always does it to perfection.

Never will we take a trip into ecstasy,

Until we live out each others fantasies.

So let me search into your soul,

And unravel your stories that are untold.

LATE NIGHT FANTASY

Its 3am, I'm awake and my loins are burning,

As I touch myself and just imagine being with you.

My desires are on fire and they are yearning,

To get inside you and do what we do.

The thoughts of caressing your breasts,

And putting them in my mouth.

Makes me go into cardiac arrest,

As I proceed to go south.

The moisture you have in between those lips,

Arouses me to such an extreme.

When my tongue hits there, you grind your hips,

Makes me work it so much, it makes you scream.

I want to call but, you're probably asleep.

Hopefully dreaming the same naughty thoughts.

I am picturing me in you so deep,

Mmmmm, the images are making me raw.

I need to feed this hunger that I have inside,

Gotta make love to you at this moment.

The feeling I get when I let you ride,

 Is beyond words with this beautiful woman.

Maybe if I text you in our usual code,

You'll understand what I am trying to say.

The thought of sexing you creates a mode,

That will last until the next day.

But to my dismay, I have made a mess.

My hands are sticky and about to dry.

With all those arousing thoughts,

I am no longer stressed.

Leaving me relieved and a peaceful sleep in my eyes.

IN THE ROMANTIC MOOD

The time has come today, only for us to say, I love you.

Just dim the lights and come here,

Let us cherish the moments my dear.

As we sit here looking at an open fire.

I know we have a burning desire.

The words we whispered in each other's ears,

Are made for us to only hear.

We sit and stare at the moving flames,

As the sparks dance in a little game.

The feelings we have become so true,

The passion that grows between me and you.

The wind blows a gentle breeze,

This seems to put your mind at ease.

As I run my fingers through your hair,

You seem like you haven't a care.

I start to make little gestures, that are like little hints.

These are moves that can't be measured,

Like the pieces of flint.

Your eyes are saying to take control,

and your lips are wet as rain.

Only to do this as a whole, and never feel any pain.

I'm waiting to remove the clothes,

to see the body Heaven knows.

As we do a dance making us feel good,

a chance knows it should.

The time has come for us to say,

I love you, I love you in so many ways.

I DON'T WANT NOBODY ELSE

I don't want nobody else, girl its true.

I don't want nobody else, only you.

Girl, I've been running you down,

Because you're the finest thing in town.

I want you to be mine all mine,

I really think that you look fine.

I see you walk the street at night,

I see you when I close my eyes.

You have a style that looks so right,

Girl won't you come and be my prize.

I don't want nobody else,

no one makes me feel so good.

I don't want nobody else,

come on baby like you know it should.

You think that I don't watch the way,

Your hips just swing and sway,

Your eyes are like a roaring flame,

So, baby quit playing games.

Don't you know , I don't want nobody else.

I don't know why? I don't want nobody else. I can't lie.

Girl, I've been hunting you down

Cause you're the finest thing in town.

I want you to be mine all mine,

I really think that you are oh so fine.

Its only you I want to know,

Its my love I'm wanting to show.

Because, I don't want nobody else, only you.

I don't want nobody else, girl its true.

LET'S MAKE LOVE

When I make love to you, I see the light.

That shines down on us so bright.

The candle burns on the dresser real slow,

Like the love we make and the love we know.

You turn to me with your body dressed in silk,

Feeling on you just makes me wilt.

Soft and ebony moving and flowing real tame,

We're making love baby, and then you call my name.

You push and pull me in wanting some more,

Bouncing from the bed then onto the floor.

Rolling around like a burning flame,

Trying to win at the love making game.

We kiss and hug and we start to neck,

Getting goose bumps with every little peck.

Let's make love until we can't move.

So sore and tired until we are black and blue.

Let's make love all through the night,

Until the sun creeps up in the light.

I want to caress your lovely thighs,

I want to reach just a little high.

I want to kiss you all up in between,

Until you relax and wilt, you know what I mean.

Don't deny me of this chance, to give a little of my romance.

Just open up and take it slow,

Because its your love I want to know.

WHEN I'M AROUND YOU

Watching you from a distance,

makes my heart skip a beat.

When you walk by it gets intense,

 the Earth moves under your feet.

The way you walk on any given day,

makes the flowers swing and sway.

When you talk to me on the phone,

I can hear in your voice you're alone.

That's just the way that I feel, When I'm around you.

I don't know what to say, When I'm around you.

Tell me what you see, When I'm around you.

What do you do, When I'm around you.

I start to lose all self-control, when I'm with you.

You fill my soul. You take away my every fear.

When I'm around you, I always shed joyful tears.

You want me to be your man,

after this I truly understand.

The reasons that are on your mind,

because I too think in time.

When I'm around you, I become unglued.

No one else has put me in this kind of mood.

When I'm around you, I feel so right.

So please just be mine tonight.

When I'm around you, you make me sweat.

Thinking about our love, I have no regrets.

I WANNA MAKE LOVE TO YOU

Turn out the lights and close the door,

Its time to make love and I want some more.

Light the candles one by one,

Just give me you and then some.

Let your hair flow down and just be wild,

Come over here and be my love child.

As we take a ride into paradise,

And do this until there no more nice.

I wanna make love to you, all night.

I wanna make love to you, until its right.

I just got to get you in my arms, and hold you tight.

I wanna make love to you, tonight.

I feel like a child at play, in a big playground.

Running over to the merry-go-round, hoping and wishing someday.

That some day in my arms you will soon lay.

Touching and kissing are things of the past,

Making true love that really lasts,

Takes time and I got plenty of that.

Hoping you will show me where it's at.

Lay your precious body on my bed, As we get between the sheets.

Toss and turn your pretty head, And lets tangle up our feet.

Let the night unwind, And let me blow your mind.

As I take you into the stratosphere,

And our love will take us away from here.

Oh how, I wanna make love to you!

WHY CAN'T WE TRY, ONE MORE TIME

I'm sitting on the back of the train,

Just thinking about all of the pain.

That we put each other through.

It seems we both found someone new.

My heart is pouring tears of shame,

That tell the story of the game.

You told me about the things you've done,

It seems like you been having a lot of fun.

I guess that he's treating you real fine,

I can't help but think of the time.

The time that you and I were one,

Now the time is over and done.

Why can't we try, one more time?

I don't understand why I let you go.

Why don't we try, one more time?

You know I loved you so much,

I just can't be away from your touch.

The rain is coming down real hard,

You can hear it pouring on the roof.

My feelings are starting to fall apart,

My emotions are truly moved.

I'm thinking about the times we spent together,

No matter what the weather.

Why can't we try, one more time?

I still feel deep inside that you're mine.

COMING HOME

I've been on the road for a long time,

Traveling many long and tiring miles.

I've seen so many roads, I'm losing my mind.

What I wouldn't give just to see your smile.

I've been every where and seen a lot of places,

Every town is different in its own way.

Every woman I see seems to have your face,

But again, its just another day.

That's why, I'm coming home, home to my baby

I'm coming home, to my loving lady.

Standing on the stage night after night,

Can be fun and exciting.

But sooner or later something doesn't feel right.

And the crowds don't seem to be as enticing.

Sometimes I get so lonely, I just feel like I could cry.

Knowing that I'm just only, Making myself about to die.

I'm coming home. I'm coming home.

Sometimes when I look out the window,

Of the plane, bus or cars.

I just wish that I could go

Way up into the stars

I'm on my way to a place I know,

Where only my heart can rest.

It is the only place I can go,

Where I know the place is the best.

I'm coming home.

I NEVER KNEW WHAT LOVE WAS

Its two o'clock in the morning.

And I'm wondering where you are.

A new day will soon be dawning,

As I adore you from a far.

I sit in my bed, with nervous feelings,

That eat me up deep inside.

Thinking that you're out stealing,

The heart of another, maybe it's my pride.

I never knew what love was, until I met you.

I tried to focus my intentions, but didn't know what to do.

If I set my spirit free; maybe you'll be here with me.

A hundred scented candles fill my room,

Each one lit to represent tonight.

Through my blinds, is the light of the moon,

Beaming the romance that'll make it right.

But as the night turns into day,

And the memory of your scent is gone.

I'll continue on in my own way,

As your voice becomes a gentle song.

I never knew what love was,

Until I received your kiss.

I never knew what love was,

Now I realize what I've missed.

QUESTIONS FROM THE HEART

Is that a tear I see, coming from our eyes?

Am I to feel sympathy, for all of your lies?

Will you ever be forgiven, for all that you've done?

Is it really worth living, why was I so dumb?

If I gave you my heart, would you throw it away?

Would you tear it apart, and have nothing to say?

Could you live with yourself, knowing that I'm hurt?

Or would you be selfish and continue to flirt?

There are more questions I need to ask.

But for now I'll let them pass.

Because you'll never give an answer I want,

Only lies and betrayal, to forever taunt.

Keeping me on a ten foot leash,

Relinquishing me from releasing the beast.

That lies deep within my very soul,

That holds a heart that has a hole.

www.ingramcontent.com/pod-product-compliance
Lightning Source LLC
LaVergne TN
LVHW040157080526
838202LV00042B/3199